Retold by
Russell Punter
Illustrated by
Barba

retold by
Susanna Davidson

C015162203

The
Tin Soldier

Based on a story by
Hans Christian Andersen

Retold by Russell Punter

Illustrated by Lorena Alvarez

Reading consultant: Alison Kelly
University of Roehampton

"Happy birthday Tom!"
said Grandpa.

Wow, thanks!

"Just what I wanted,"
Tom cried, "tin soldiers!"

"Oh dear! This soldier only has one leg," said Grandpa.

Attention!

Quick, march!

Tom didn't mind.
He spent all day playing.

3

At bedtime, he packed the
soldiers back in their box.

But the one-legged soldier
was missing.

"Where's he gone?"
wondered Tom.

Don't worry.

"You can look for him
tomorrow," said Grandpa.

Tom's other toys waited until he was asleep.

The soldiers tried to join in.
But they were stuck in their
box...

...except for the
one-legged soldier.

He had fallen behind a
pile of toy building blocks.

But he didn't join in
the games.

He was gazing at the
fairytale palace in
the corner.

It once belonged to
Tom's sister.

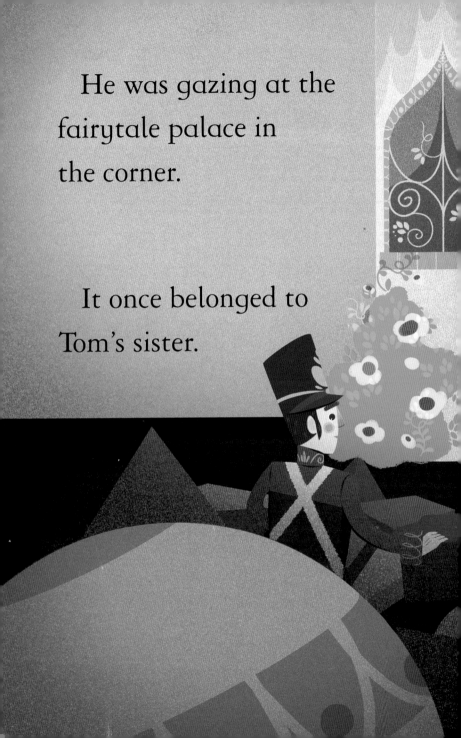

A paper ballerina doll
stood in the doorway.

The pretty ballerina was
dancing on one leg.

"She'd be a perfect wife for
me," said the soldier.

The soldier ignored him.
He smiled at the ballerina.

She smiled back.

The jealous jack-in-the-box
turned bright red.

"Just wait," he fumed.

The next morning, Tom
found his missing soldier.

He put him by
the window.

The cruel jack-in-the-box
saw his chance.

He took a deep breath, and blew as hard as he could.

The tin soldier fell
out of the window...

"Ow!" cried the soldier.

He tried to move. But his
foot was stuck.

Two boys ran up.

"Look!" shouted one.

"A tin soldier."

"Let's turn him into a sailor," said the other.

They made a little boat out of an old newspaper.

They stood the tin soldier
in the boat.

Then they dropped it in
the gutter.

The soldier's boat sailed along the street.

But things were about
to get worse.

There was a drain hole in
the road ahead.

The paper boat shot down the drain.

It landed, splosh, in a dirty, smelly sewer.

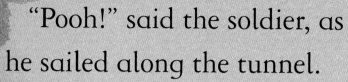
"Pooh!" said the soldier, as
he sailed along the tunnel.

He turned the bend. A fat
black rat was in his way.

"Pay me a penny to pass!"
ordered the rat.

The soldier had no money.
He couldn't stop anyway.

The soldier sailed on
and on.

"Will I ever see the
ballerina doll again?"
he wondered.

Just then, he noticed
daylight up ahead.

Seconds later, the boat
whooshed out of the sewer.

The tin soldier was glad to be out of the sewer.

But he wasn't happy for long. Now his boat was leaking.

The next moment, he was sinking like a stone.

And things were about to get worse.

A huge fish swam by.

It swallowed the tin soldier in one gulp.

The soldier sat sadly in the fish's tummy.

But his luck was about to change.

A man caught the fish.

What a beauty!

He took it to sell at the market.

Tom's Grandpa bought
the fish.

He carried it home
for supper.

He unwrapped the fish...

Bonk!

and the tin soldier fell out.

Grandpa took the tin
soldier to Tom's room.

"Welcome home, soldier!"
shouted Tom.

All the toys were glad
to see the tin soldier...

except one.

Grrrr!

He went hopping mad...

broke his
spring...

and never
worked again.

The very next day, the
tin soldier married the
lovely ballerina.

And they invited all the
toys to a noisy party.

After Tom was asleep,
of course.

About the story

The Steadfast Tin Soldier was first written
by Hans Christian Andersen in 1838.
The original version had a very sad ending.
The tin soldier and the paper ballerina melted
in a fireplace. All that was left of them was a
heart-shaped piece of tin and a black sequin.

Series editor: Lesley Sims

First published in 2012 by Usborne Publishing Ltd., Usborne House,
83-85 Saffron Hill, London EC1N 8RT, England. www.usborne.com
Copyright © 2012 Usborne Publishing Ltd.

USBORNE FIRST READING
Level Four

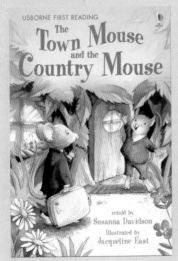

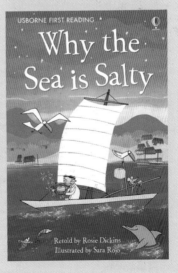